Dr Xargle's
Book of Earth Tiggers

Translated into Human by
JEANNE WILLIS

Pictures by
TONY ROSS

Andersen Press

Good morning, class.

Today we are going to learn about Earth Tiggers.
Earth Tiggers are made of furry material.
This does up underneath with pink buttons.

They are available in Patterned or Plain.

Press them in the middle to find the squeaker.

Earth Tiggers grow sharp thorns.
These they use to carve objects made of wood.

Or to climb steep Earthlets.

Earth Tiggers like gardening. They dig a hole
and plant a stinkpod. This never grows.

During the rainy season, stinkpods may be planted
in any container found in the earthdwelling.

Earth Tiggers like breakfast at 5 a.m. Precisely.
They massage the pyjamas of the sleeping Earthlet.
They sit on his nostrils.

Earth Tiggers eat meatblob.

This they collect on their many antennae to save for later.

A healthy Earth Tigger also needs cowjuice, tandoori cluck bird, muckworm and old green gibble in dustbin gravy.

Earth Tiggers can hear a parcel of pigrolls being
opened five earth miles away.

They cannot hear an Earthlet shouting "Tiddles!"
in the next garden.

Earth Tiggers hate the Earth Hound.
They fold in half and puff air into their waggler.
Then they go into orbit with a hiss and a crackle.

In a glass capsule full of stones and vegetables lives
the sparkly, golden fishstick.

This the Earth Tigger likes. He puts his mitten into
the water and mixes the fishstick all about.

Earth Tiggers like to sing loudly in the moonlight with their friends.
The Earthling hurls items of footwear all around.

Earth Tiggers sometimes put hairy pudding on the stairs.
The Earthling is made to step on this with no socks on.

Repeat this phrase after me:
"Whoops, I have slipped on a furball and broken both my legs."

Sometimes the Earth Tigger gets torn and must be taken to the menders
First he must be caught and wrapped in cardboard and string.
The Earthlet sticks himself back together with pink paper.

When Earth Tiggers are born, the Earthlet gives them a bed made from knitted twigs and a bag of birdfluff. This the Tiggerlets hate.

They go to sleep in the headdress of the Earthling.

For Wilbur, Fatty and Sue

This paperback edition published in 2011 by Andersen Press Ltd.
First published in Great Britain in 1990 by Andersen Press Ltd., 20 Vauxhall Bridge Road, London SW1V 2SA.
Published in Australia by Random House Australia Pty., Level 3, 100 Pacific Highway, North Sydney, NSW 2060.
Text copyright © Jeanne Willis, 1990. Illustration copyright © Tony Ross, 1990.
The rights of Jeanne Willis and Tony Ross to be identified as the author and illustrator of this work
have been asserted by them in accordance with the Copyright, Designs and Patents Act, 1988.
All rights reserved. Colour separated in Switzerland by Photolitho AG, Zürich.
Printed and bound in Singapore by Tien Wah Press.
Tony Ross has used pen, ink and watercolour in this book.

10   9   8   7   6   5   4   3   2   1

British Library Cataloguing in Publication Data available.

ISBN 978 1 84939 297 6
ISBN 978 1 84939 365 2 (The Book People)

This book has been printed on acid-free paper

MORE Dr Xargle BOOKS:

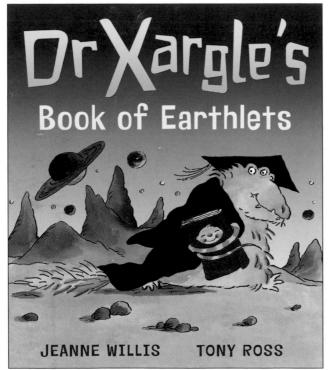

9781849392921

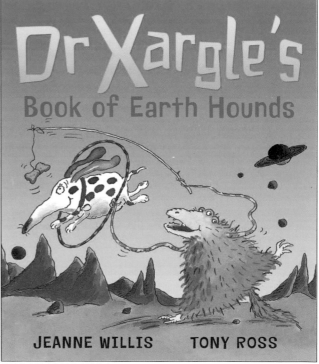

9781842701706